10
Minute Tales

MR. MEN
Roger Hargreaves

D0246197

MR. BUMP LOSES HIS MEMORY

When you see these symbols:

Read aloud	**Read alone**	**Read along**
Read aloud to your child.	Support your child as they read alone.	Read along with your child.

Read aloud Read along

Mr Bump was the sort of person
who was always having accidents.

If there was something for Mr Bump to
bump into, break, crash or drop, he would.

When he had his breakfast, he would spill
the tea all over the table, and the salt
all over his eggs.

Poor Mr Bump.

Read alone

Mr Bump was the sort of person who was always having accidents.

He would have small accidents.

When Mr Bump cleaned the downstairs windows, he would use a small ladder.

CRASH! went the kitchen window as he rested the ladder against it.

"Oh dear," thought Mr Bump.

Then he fell off the ladder.

BUMP!

Read alone

He had small accidents.

Read aloud   Read along

He would have medium-sized accidents.

When he cleaned the upstairs windows, he would use a long ladder.

CRASH! went the living room window as he turned the corner of the path.

"Oh dear," thought Mr Bump again.

CRASH! went the bedroom window as he rested the ladder against it.

Read alone

He had medium-sized accidents.

Read aloud   Read along

And he would have big accidents.

When his chimney pot came loose in a storm, Mr Bump decided to fix it.

He fetched a very long ladder from his garden shed. Mr Bump rested the ladder against the wall of his house so he could climb up onto the roof and mend the chimney pot.

CRASH! went the chimney pot.

Mr Bump had lots and lots of accidents.

Read alone

And he had **big** accidents!
Lots and lots of accidents.

One day, Mr Bump got out of bed,
or rather, he fell out of bed as he did
every morning.

He drew back the curtains and opened
the window.

It was a beautiful day.

He leant on the window sill, breathed in
deeply and ... fell out of the window.

BUMP!

One day, Mr Bump got out of bed ...
and fell out of the window. BUMP!

Read aloud   Read along

Mr Bump sat up and rubbed his head. And as he rubbed, it dawned on him that he had no idea where he was.

He had no idea whose garden he was sitting in.

He had no idea whose house he was sitting in front of.

And he had no idea who he was.

Mr Bump had lost his memory.

Read alone

He rubbed his head. Mr Bump had no idea
who he was. He had lost his memory.

Read aloud   Read along

Mr Bump walked up to his garden gate and looked down the lane.

Mr Muddle was passing by.

"Good afternoon," said Mr Muddle.

As you and I know, it was morning. But Mr Muddle, not surprisingly, always gets things in a muddle.

"I seem to have lost my memory," said Mr Bump. "Do you know what my name is?"

"You're Mr Careful," said Mr Muddle.

"Thank you," said Mr Bump.

Mr Bump asked Mr Muddle who he was.
Mr Muddle said that he was Mr Careful.

Read aloud   Read along

Mr Bump went into town.

The first person he met was Mrs Packet the grocer, who was carrying an armful of groceries.

"Hello," said Mr Bump, "I'm Mr Careful. Can I help?"

"Just the person! I need someone careful to deliver these eggs."

Read alone

So Mr Bump thought he was Mr Careful. He agreed to deliver Mrs Packet's eggs for her.

Mr Bump took the eggs from
Mrs Packet and set off down the
high street.

And because he was Mr Bump, he slipped
and fell on the eggs, breaking all of them.

CRACK!

"You're not all that careful, are you?"
said Mrs Packet.

"Sorry," said Mr Bump.

Read alone

But he slipped and broke all the eggs.
CRACK!

He walked on past the dairy.
Mr Bottle the manager came out.

"I'm looking for someone to drive the
milk float," he said. "What's your name?"

"Mr Careful," replied Mr Bump.

"Perfect," said Mr Bottle. "I need someone
careful to deliver the milk."

Mr Bump agreed to deliver the milk
for Mr Bottle from the dairy.

Read aloud   Read along

Mr Bump set off down the road.

As he turned the corner, he hit the curb and the milk float turned over, smashing all the milk bottles.

SMASH!

"Well, that wasn't very carefully done, was it?" said Mr Bottle.

"Sorry," said Mr Bump.

Read alone

But Mr Bump crashed the milk float and broke all the milk bottles. SMASH!

Then he met Mr Brush the painter,
who was up a ladder, painting.

"Hello," said Mr Bump. "I'm Mr Careful.
Do you need a hand?"

"Yes please," replied Mr Brush. "I need
someone careful to pass me my
paint pot."

Read alone

Then he agreed to pass some paint
to Mr Brush the painter.

Read aloud **Read along**

Mr Bump began to climb
the ladder.

But, being Mr Bump, he fell off and
the pot of paint landed on his head.

SPLASH!

But Mr Bump fell off the ladder and the pot of paint landed on his head. SPLASH!

Read aloud   Read along

Mr Bump went for a walk.

"I don't understand it," he said to himself. "My name is Mr Careful, but I can't do anything carefully!"

It was then that he walked into a tree.

And bumped his head.

BUMP!

Read alone

Mr Bump was confused. He went for a walk and bumped his head on a tree. BUMP!

Read aloud   Read along

An apple fell out of the tree into his hand.

"That's odd," he said to himself. "How did I get here? The last thing I remember is opening my bedroom window."

"... And where did all this paint come from?"

You know, don't you?

Just at that moment Farmer Fields turned up. "Careful!" he called.

"That sounds familiar," said Mr Bump, and he fell down the bank into the river!

Read alone

He was now Mr Bump again. "Careful," said Farmer Fields, but Mr Bump fell into the river!

MR. MEN™
LITTLE MISS™

Roger Hargreaves

OVER 80 BOOKS TO COLLECT

MR. TICKLE	LITTLE MISS PRINCESS	MR. HAPPY	LITTLE MISS SUNSHINE	MR. BUMP	LITTLE MISS TROUBLE
MR. GREEDY	LITTLE MISS NAUGHTY	MR. NOSEY	LITTLE MISS HELPFUL	MR. SNEEZE	LITTLE MISS NEAT

START COLLECTING TODAY!

www.egmont.co.uk

EGMONT